The Sea Monster

Margaret Ryan

Illustrated by

It was Saturday afternoon and everyone in Barney's house was busy.

Mum was in the kitchen making a fish pie.

Dad was in the sitting room
making a model ship. And Tess,
Barney's big sister, was in the hall
making a phone call to her friend.

Barney was in his bedroom
making a mess.

He made a really messy sea monster and painted it black. It had a black, shiny body, a black, shiny head and a black, shiny tail. Then he remembered a sea monster joke.

"I'll show my sea monster to the others," he said. "And I'll tell them my joke."

Barney went downstairs to the kitchen. His mum was still making her pie.

"Mum, Mum," he said, shaking her elbow. "Look at the black, shiny sea monster I've made."

"Oh Barney," said his mum. "You've made me drop the fish."

"Sorry," said Barney. "But listen to my joke. What do sea monsters like to eat?"

But his mum was too busy to listen.

"I know," said Barney. "I'll show my sea monster to Dad, and tell him my joke."

He went into the sitting room. His dad was still making his model ship.

"Dad, Dad," said Barney, shaking his elbow. "Look at the black, shiny sea monster I've made."

"Oh Barney," said his dad. "You've made me drop the mast."

"Sorry," said Barney. "But listen to my joke. What do sea monsters like to eat?"

But his dad was too busy to listen.

"I know," said Barney. "I'll show
my sea monster to Tess, and tell her
my joke."

He went into the hall. His sister
was still making her phone call.

"Tess, Tess," said Barney, shaking her elbow. "Look at the black, shiny sea monster I've made."

"Go away you little monster," said Tess. "You've made me drop the phone."

"Sorry," said Barney. "But listen to my joke. What do sea monsters like to eat?"

But Tess was too busy to listen.

11

Barney went back upstairs to his bedroom.

"It's not fair," he said. "No one wants to look at my sea monster or listen to my joke."

He put his hands on his chin and looked out of his window at the big river that flowed past his house. The river was quiet.

Then suddenly, something in the river moved. Something big and black and shiny. It rose in and out of the water. In and out. In and out.

"Oh no," said Barney. "It's a *real* sea monster. I must tell the others."

He ran downstairs to the kitchen.

"Mum, Mum," he cried. "There's a real sea monster in the river. Come and look."

"Oh Barney," said his mum.
"I haven't got time for your jokes just now. Can't you see I'm busy?"

Barney ran into the sitting room.

"Dad, Dad," he cried. "There's a real sea monster in the river. Come and look."

"Oh Barney," said his dad.
"I haven't got time for your jokes just now. Can't you see I'm busy?"

Barney ran into the hall.

"Tess, Tess," he cried. "There's a real sea monster in the river. Come and look."

"Go away you little monster," said Tess. "I haven't got time for your jokes just now. Can't you see I'm busy?"

"It's not a joke," yelled Barney so that everyone could hear. "It's a real sea monster."

But no one would come and look.

Barney ran back upstairs and
looked out of his window at the river.
The big, black, shiny sea monster
was still there.

"It's not fair," said Barney. "No one
will believe me."

Then he heard Tess put the phone down, and that gave him an idea.

"I know who'll believe me," he said, and he went to the phone and dialled 999.

"Police, please," he said. "I've just seen a sea monster in the river."

The police believed Barney. They had seen the sea monster too.

"But it's not a sea monster, Barney," they said. "It's a little lost whale. We've never had one in the river before. We're going to play him some whale sounds and lead him back out to sea."

Soon Barney's street was full of people who had come to see the little whale.

"See," said Barney, pointing it out to his family. "It looks just like the sea monster I made."

"Poor little whale," said his mum.
"I wonder if he likes fish pie."

"I could make a model of him to
swim beside my ship," said his dad.

"The little whale is big news," said
his sister. "I must phone all my friends."

"I know what I'm going to do," said Barney. "I'm going to tell the little whale my joke."

And he called out across the river. "Little whale, listen to my joke. What do sea monsters like to eat?"

The little whale listened.

"Fish and *ships*!" said Barney.

The little whale didn't say
anything, but he flipped his black,
shiny tail, and Barney was sure he
saw him smile.